D1076135

PIPPBROOK BOOKS

First published in the UK in 1999 by Templar Publishing
This softback edition published in the UK in 2015 by Pippbrook Books,
an imprint of Templar Publishing,
part of the Bonnier Publishing Group,
The Plaza, 535 King's Road, London, SW10 0SZ
www.templarco.co.uk
www.bonnierpublishing.com

Copyright © 1999 by The Templar Company Limited

3 5 7 9 10 8 6 4 2

All rights reserved

ISBN 978-1-84877-763-7

Designed by Hayley Bebb and Manhar Chauhan
Edited by Dugald Steer and Liza Miller

Printed in Malaysia

PIPPBROOK
BOOKS

The BRAVE Little OWL

WRITTEN BY GILL DAVIES   ILLUSTRATIONS BY DICK TWINNEY

Little Owl fluffs up his soft, furry feathers.

His bright, round eyes peep out of the nest.
Then he squeaks. He squeaks because
he is afraid of the dark outside.

The fox cubs laugh as they play below.
"Owls are meant to like night-time best," they tease.

"What a funny little owl!" laugh the squirrels.

"An odd little owl," giggle the moths.

"A very strange owl," agree the rabbits,
"to be frightened of the dark."

Mother Owl tries to comfort Little Owl.
"Be brave, Little Owl," she says.
"Look at the stars. See how beautiful they are."

"Be brave, Little Owl. Look at the moon.
See how big and golden it is," says Father Owl.

But Little Owl buries his head under his wing.

It is time for Little Owl to learn to fly.
He sits on the branches of the tree with
the other baby owls in a wobbling row.
The breeze blows their feathers
and the leaves whisper.
The other forest creatures come to watch.

Little Owl is terrified. He closes his eyes.
Then, suddenly, he hears a night-bird singing.
The music is beautiful.

He hears a waterfall splashing.
The sound is exciting.

He wants to hear more and he forgets to be afraid.

Little Owl edges along the branch to hear better.
His eyes are still shut tight, so he does not see that
he has reached the end of the branch...

...WHOOSH!

Little Owl tumbles down in a blur of feathers.
Be brave, Little Owl!

Little Owl spreads his wings to try and balance.
The warm breeze scoops him up and holds him gentl
Little Owl flaps his wings. Little Owl is flying!
He opens his big, round eyes in amazement.

All the forest animals cheer!

Little Owl opens his big, round eyes even wider.
He flies above the forest.
He flies across the golden moon.
He flies past the sparkling, glittering stars.

Little Owl flies down and perches on his branch.

He looks out over the trees,
listening to the sounds of the forest creatures.

He looks out over the lake, which is
sparkling with reflections of the moon and stars.

Brave Little Owl sees that the night
is not so dark after all.

Brave Little Owl sees how bright the night is.
It is beautiful!
"Tu-whit tu-whoo," sings Brave Little Owl,
and he flies off into the shining, silver night.